I Don't Like
Chocolate

by Jackie Walter and Alex Naidoo

W
FRANKLIN WATTS
LONDON•SYDNEY

I don't like chocolate.

3

I don't like sweets.

I don't like sandwiches.

I don't like crisps.

I don't like popcorn.

11

I don't like biscuits.

13

I don't like ice cream.

I don't like grapes.

I don't like peas.

Story trail

Start at the beginning of the story trail. Ask your child to retell the story in their own words, pointing to each picture in turn to recall the sequence of events.

Start

Independent Reading

This series is designed to provide an opportunity for your child to read on their own. These notes are written for you to help your child choose a book and to read it independently.

In school, your child's teacher will often be using reading books which have been banded to support the process of learning to read. Use the book band colour your child is reading in school to help you make a good choice. *I Don't Like Chocolate* is a good choice for children reading at Pink 1B in their classroom to read independently.

The aim of independent reading is to read this book with ease, so that your child enjoys the story and relates it to their own experiences.

About the book

In this story, a little girl wants to share her food with the animals, but they don't like the same things as she does.

Before reading

Help your child to learn how to make good choices by asking: "Why did you choose this book? Why do you think you will enjoy it?" Support your child to think about what they already know about the story context. Look at the cover together and ask: "What do you think the story will be about?" Read the title aloud and ask: "Who do you think doesn't like chocolate?"

Remind your child that they can try to sound out the letters to make a word if they get stuck.

Decide together whether your child will read the story independently or read it aloud to you. When books are short, as at Pink 1B, your child may wish to do both!

.Watts
.blished in Great Britain in 2019 by The Watts Publishing Group

.right © The Watts Publishing Group 2019

.ries Editors: Jackie Hamley and Melanie Palmer
.eries Advisors: Dr Sue Bodman and Glen Franklin
Series Designers: Cathryn Gilbert and Peter Scoulding

A CIP catalogue record for this book is
available from the British Library.

ISBN 978 1 4451 6754 1 (hbk)
ISBN 978 1 4451 6755 8 (pbk)
ISBN 978 1 4451 6753 4 (library ebook)

Printed in China

Franklin Watts
An imprint of
Hachette Children's Group
Part of The Watts Publishing Group
Carmelite House
50 Victoria Embankment
London EC4Y 0DZ

An Hachette UK Company
www.hachette.co.uk

www.franklinwatts.co.uk